How do I use this scheme?

Key Words with Peter and Jane has three
parallel series, each containing twelve books. All three
series are written using the same carefully controlled
vocabulary. Readers will get the most out of **Key Words** with
Peter and Jane when they follow the books in the pattern
1a, 1b, 1c; 2a, 2b, 2c and so on.

• Series a
gradually introduces and repeats new words.

• Series b
provides further practice of these same words, but
in a different context and with different illustrations.

• Series c
uses familiar words to teach **phonics** in a methodical way,
enabling children to read increasingly difficult words.
It also provides a link to writing.

LADYBIRD BOOKS

UK | USA | Canada | Ireland | Australia
India | New Zealand | South Africa

Ladybird Books is part of the Penguin Random House group of companies
whose addresses can be found at global.penguinrandomhouse.com.

www.penguin.co.uk   www.puffin.co.uk   www.ladybird.co.uk

First published 1964
This edition 2009, 2014, 2016
Copyright © Ladybird Books Ltd, 1964
001

ISBN: 978-1-409-30118-9

Printed in China

Key Words

with Peter and Jane

3b   Boys and girls

written by W. Murray
illustrated by M. Aitchison

Peter and Jane are
at home.

They are at play.

Look at this, says Peter.

We like to jump.

We can jump on this.

We can have some fun
on this.

at   play   on

Peter and Jane like
to play.

I want to jump on this,
says Peter.

Look at me, Jane.

Look at me.

Up I go.

Up and up I go.

It's fun to play on this.

---

me   Up   up

Jane wants to play.

I want to play, please,
Jane says.

Peter, I want to jump,
please.

Jane jumps up and down.

Up and down I go,
Jane says.

Up and down, up and
down.

Look at me, Peter.

---

please   down

Peter likes to help.

He sees Daddy go up.

He wants to help Daddy.

I want to help you,
he says.

Please can I help you?

Yes, says Daddy, you can
help me.

---

help   sees   Daddy

Here comes Jane with
some tea.

This is for you, Daddy,
Jane says.

Here you are. Here's
some tea for you. Come
down for the tea, please.

Daddy sees Jane with the
tea, and comes down.

---

with   tea

Here's Daddy with some apples.

Peter has an apple, and Jane has an apple.

Peter and Jane see Daddy go up and down.

They want to help Daddy with the apples.

---

an   apple   apples

Peter and Jane are in the car with Daddy.

They like it in the car.

Mummy is at home.

They see a toy shop and a sweet shop.

Peter wants to see the school.

car   Mummy   school

They go on to the school.

Here it is, says Peter,
here's the school.

Peter and Jane like the
school.

Here's a cake shop,
says Daddy.

Mummy wants some cakes.

We have to get cakes
for tea.

cake   cakes   get

Here we are at home, says Daddy.

Peter helps Daddy with the car, and Jane helps Mummy get the tea.

Good girl, says Mummy to Jane.

You are a good girl to help me like this.

Good   good   girl

Jane and Peter like to play with the rabbits.

Peter has one, and Jane has one.

They are good to the rabbits.

Peter's rabbit can jump, and Jane's rabbit can jump.

The rabbits like Peter and Jane.

rabbit   rabbits   one

Here's a home for the rabbits.

Daddy helps Peter with it, and the dog looks on.

It's Pat. He's a good dog.

Pat likes rabbits.

He likes to play with the rabbits.

Peter and Jane have some flowers.

Jane says, Girls like flowers.

Peter says, Yes, and boys like flowers.

Jane wants to have a flower shop.

Peter helps with it.

He gets some red flowers for Jane.

---

flowers   boys   red

Here's a tree, says Jane, and here are some flowers.

Come and look, Peter.

Look at the red flowers and the tree.

Peter looks.

Yes, he says, I like the tree and I like the flowers.

This is a boat, says Peter, a boat on the water.

Here's a man in a boat.

A boy is with the man.

Have a look, Jane.

Have a look at this red boat on the water.

boat   man

I want a boat, says Peter.

I want one to play with.

Please help me, Daddy.

Please help me with this.

I want some help with this.

Yes, says Daddy, I want to help you with the boat.

Here's Peter with the boat.

It's a red one.

He wants to go to the water with the boat.

Daddy gets the car to go to the water.

Jane is in the car.

Here they are, at the water.

Peter is in the water with the red boat.

He has fun in the water with the boat.

Can you see a fish in the water? says Jane.

No, says Peter.

Peter sees a man and a boy.

The man has a boat.

It's a Police boat.

Peter says to Jane,
Look at that boat.

That man has a Police boat.

I like that Police boat.

Police   that

This is the school.

The boys and girls are at school.

Here are the Police.

The Police are at the school.

They have come in a Police car.

They have come to help the boys and girls.

Peter has a toy car.

Jane is with Peter.

Jane says, Here's a shop with apples.

Please get some apples, Peter.

Go into this shop for some apples.

Yes, we want some apples, says Peter.

Peter and Jane want to go
to the station to see
the trains.

They like to look at the
trains at the station.

Here they go, on a bus
to the station.

It's a red bus.

They like it on the bus.

station   train   trains   bus

The bus has come to the station.

Peter and Jane go into the station.

They like to see the trains.

I like to go on a train with Mummy and Daddy, says Jane.

Yes, it's fun to go on a train, says Peter.

The boy and the girl are at home.

It was fun at the station, says Jane.

Yes, it was fun to see the trains, says Peter.

He gives a ball to Pat.

Mummy gives Peter an apple, and gives some cakes to Jane.

was   gives

The toys go in here,
says Jane.

Mummy says, You have
to go to bed, Jane.

You have to go to bed,
Peter.

Come on, up to bed
you go.

You are a good girl, Jane,
and you are a good
boy, Peter.

bed

New words used in this book

Total number of new words: 36
Average repetition per word: 11